D0118649

Robins

To Ruthie

Robins
Songbirds of Spring

Mia Posada

Carolrhoda Books, Inc. / Minneapolis

One early spring morning,
bright and clear,
in a budding tree,
a robin appears.

It has a rusty red breast
under brownish gray wings.

It hops
from branch

to branch

as it sings.

Soon the spring air
is alive with the sounds
of robins returned
from their wintering grounds.

"Cheer-up cheerily," they sing at dawn,

pecking their beaks at a damp morning lawn.

They dig up insects and worms
from the earth below

**and find trees on which
tasty berries grow.**

A male and female robin
search for a nesting site.
The sheltered branch of a
maple tree seems just right.

The female robin collects weeds
from nearby gardens.
Then she adds mud,
which dries and hardens.

Soft grass collected from the ground
lines the nest, cozy and round.

Soon in the
nest, three
little eggs lie.

They are light blue,
the color of sky.

The mother robin protects the eggs from cold and storm by sitting on them to keep them warm.

In twelve days,
there are sounds
of tapping and scratching.

Cracks form in the eggs.
The chicks are hatching!

First come
their beaks,
then tiny
pink legs.

The chicks work
hard to break free
from their eggs.

The newly
hatched chicks
look tired and wet.
Their eyes are not
even open yet.

The mother and father robins take turns
feeding their chicks
insects and worms.

After two weeks, the chicks have spotted orange breasts. Now called fledglings, they prepare to leave the nest.

The father robin
teaches the fledglings to fly

and how to find food,
such as berries, nearby.

By summer's end, the fledglings are almost full-grown.

They fly and sing and catch food on their own.

When cooler, shorter days
mark the onset of fall,
it becomes hard to find any food at all.

Upon the arrival
of winter snow and sleet,

robins travel south
in search of food to eat.

But on an early spring morning,
bright and clear,

the singing robins will reappear.

More about Robins

The American robin is one of the most common birds in North America. They live in cities, suburbs, and forests throughout all of North America, from Alaska to Mexico. Robins belong to the family of birds called thrushes. The scientific name for the American robin is *Turdus migratorius*. Early English colonists in North America gave the robin its name. It reminded the colonists of the similar, but smaller, English robin.

Robins have rust or red-orange breast feathers. This is why robins have been nicknamed "robin redbreast." Male robins have a darker shade of gray on their heads and tails than the females. Robins usually grow from 9 to 11 inches long.

The robins' main food source is berries. They also eat insects, such as caterpillars and beetles. Robins like to eat earthworms as well, which they pluck from the ground with their beaks.

In the spring, robins mate. Male robins sing to attract female partners. Each female robin builds a nest to hold her eggs. She may build it in a tree, on a windowsill, or even in a hidden spot on the ground. The female robin lays 2 to 5 eggs that hatch after 11 to 14 days. The new chicks are fed worms by their parents. The chicks stay in the nest for about

2 weeks. Then they are ready to live on their own. At this stage, they are called fledglings.

When winter comes, some robins head to warmer climates, where food is more plentiful. Robins that live in Alaska, Canada, and the northern United States travel south, or migrate. They make this long journey in groups, flying all day and resting at night. They spend the winter in the southern United States or Mexico.

In the springtime, around March, the robins return to their northern homes. They usually fly back to the same place each year. The robins' arrival signals the beginning of spring.

Watching Robins

You can learn more about robins by carefully watching, or observing, robins that you see near your home.

When you see a robin, observe its appearance. Does it have the dark gray head of a male robin or the lighter coloring of a female? Is it an adult or a young fledgling? How can you tell?

Observe the robin's behavior. Is it hopping around in the grass? Does it peck at the ground with its beak? If you see a robin carrying grass or twigs in its mouth, what do you think it may be doing?

Observing a nest is a fun way to learn firsthand about robins. If you find a robin's nest, be very careful not to go too close to the nest or to disturb the robins. It's OK to watch, but never try to touch the eggs or chicks.

Have you heard a robin singing? Only male robins sing. Their song sounds like "cheer-up cheerily."

Besides singing, robins make other sounds called calls. These are short, simple sounds. For example, a robin may call "cheep" when it feels alarmed. Next time you see a robin that is making sounds, observe the robin. What is it doing? What time of year is it? Could it be a male robin that is singing to attract a female mate? Soon you may be able to recognize the sounds of a robin even before you see it.

Attracting Robins to Your Yard

You can attract robins to your yard by supplying food, water, or a safe place to nest.

With the help of an adult, you can set up a bird feeder. Robins prefer to feed from a flat tray or platform feeder. You can build a simple one with instructions you can find in books, or you can buy one. Bird feeders are usually attached to a pole or hung above the ground from a tree. This keeps squirrels away from the birds' food. Robins love to

eat fruit, so a good way to attract them to your feeder is with pieces of apple, pear, or orange, or with berries such as blueberries or cranberries. Robins do not like to eat bird-seed. Their bodies cannot digest it easily.

Robins need water as well. If you do not have a birdbath, you can fill a clean garbage can lid with fresh water and lay it on the ground.

You can provide a safe place for robins to build their nest by setting up a nesting box. This is usually a wooden box with one open side that gives the robins a good view of their surroundings. An adult may be able to help you build a nesting box. You can find instructions for building a robin's nesting box in books or on the Internet. You can also buy nesting boxes at stores that sell bird supplies. A robin's nesting box should be hung on a wall or tree trunk 6 to 10 feet above the ground. It should be placed in a hidden spot so that it is safe from cats and birds that prey on the eggs and chicks. Putting the nesting box within view of a window is a good way for you to be able to observe it easily. Just remember to be very careful not to disturb the nest.

Carolrhoda Books, Inc.
A division of Lerner Publishing Group
241 First Avenue North
Minneapolis, MN 55401 U.S.A.

Website address: www.carolrhodabooks.com

Library of Congress Cataloging-in-Publication Data

Posada, Mia.
    Robins : songbirds of spring / written and illustrated by Mia Posada.
        p.   cm.
    Summary: Rhyming text explains the behavior and life cycle of robins.
    ISBN: 1–57505–615–1 (lib. bdg. : alk. paper)
    1. Robins—Juvenile literature. [1. Robins.] I. Title.
    QL696.P288P65   2004
    598.8'42—dc21   2003006414

Manufactured in the United States of America
1 2 3 4 5 6 – JR – 09 08 07 06 05 04